To Amy
From Lisa
Spearmon
6-12-75

Other Babar Books

Beginner Book

Pop-Up Books

BABAR
VISITS ANOTHER PLANET

Written and Illustrated by
LAURENT DE BRUNHOFF

Translated from the French by Merle Haas

Random House, Inc., New York, N.Y.

The weather is beautiful in the country of the elephants. Babar and Celeste have decided to go on a picnic with Pom, Flora and Alexander. Of course Arthur is going with them, too, and so is the little monkey, Zephir. They're all in very high spirits.

Suddenly Arthur looks up and exclaims, "Look, a rocket! There . . . behind the palm trees! I can see it; it's going to land!"

But Babar only laughs at him. "Come, come, Arthur. You're dreaming, my boy. . . . Oh! Wait a minute, you're right. It *is* a real rocket! It's coming toward us!"

The rocket lands
close beside them
with a loud WHIRR.
But what's going on? Suddenly a strong wind picks the elephants
up like feathers, and sucks them right into the cabin of the rocket. The
door closes before they have time to realize what is happening to them.
The rocket carries them off into space.

Celeste is frantic. Babar tries to calm her fears, but he himself is also worried. He wonders, "Where is this rocket taking us? There is no pilot on board. It must be guided by remote control from some other planet." Arthur, amazed, gazes through the porthole at the stars, while Pom, Flora and Alexander eat some biscuits held out to them by an automatic arm. Soft, gay music drifts into the cabin to reassure the travelers.

"What an adventure!" moans Celeste.

The trip is long, but fortunately they are comfortable. They have already passed the moon and the planet Mars. The rocket continues on still farther. At last, after many days, it nears a reddish planet.

"According to my calculations,"
says Babar, "this planet is unknown.
Whatever will we find here?"

Finally, the rocket lands. The door opens automatically. Babar climbs down the ladder and cautiously puts one foot down on the ground. "Oh, dear," he shouts. "I'm stuck and can't get my shoe up!"

Arthur bursts out laughing. "Maybe this planet is made of caramel," he suggests. But then he suddenly calls out:

"Look! Some of the inhabitants are approaching."

Driven by some strange-looking people, a fleet of skimmercraft draw near the rocket. Babar abandons his shoe, steps back up on the ladder and says to Arthur, "They must be the ones responsible for lifting us into the rocket. . . . They do not appear menacing."

As a matter of fact, the odd-looking strangers greet the new arrivals in a most friendly manner and speak as with one voice, which sounds like a clarinet. Babar calls to Celeste, "Come and see the inhabitants of this soft planet! They look like elephants, but yet they're not elephants."

These strange fellows invite Babar and Celeste to get in next to them. And then they take them to some platforms where they moor their craft. Next, some flying eggs float down from the sky and the curly-eared elephants seat themselves on small stools hung underneath. "Quick," says Babar. "Let's follow them! These flying eggs must surely be taxis."

"Courage, Celeste!" calls Babar, as he balances himself, sitting on the edge of his perch. "Now it's our turn!" cry Pom, Flora and Alexander. They're all excited and having a great time.

Carrying the entire Babar family, the flying eggs rise high in the sky. And suddenly a city appears, hanging in the air from enormous balloons. Lightly and silently, it floats above the soft planet. "This is very ingenious," Babar observes. "What an obvious idea! How else could you

live here? The houses would sink into the marshes of shifting sand."
Celeste is so astonished that she forgets to be dizzy. Above them,
Arthur calls across to his friend Zephir, "This planet is amazing, isn't
it, Zephir."

They land gently on a terrace. The natives rush up to look them over. One, wearing a pointed hat, approaches Babar and makes an interminably long speech; while another, wearing a hat shaped like a mushroom, smiles nearby. *"Toc, tuyup tuyup. Pitouit toc, loc toc!"*

Of course, Babar doesn't understand a word, but he guesses that Mr. Pointed Hat is inviting him to visit the town. Before following them on the slides, Babar replies: "Sir, one doesn't just pick people up in a rocket like this without warning!" But the curly-eared elephants don't understand what *he's* saying either.

In the house belonging to Pointed Hat and Blue Mushroom, there is a swimming pool in the living room. "Truly," says Arthur, "these elephants with curly ears know how to live." He plunges at once into the water, along with Pom and Alexander. Flora has no desire to swim in the pool. She has found a friend—a little dog with blue spots. Meanwhile, Babar and Celeste try to talk to Pointed Hat by means of many gestures. They almost succeed in having a real conversation.

In the evening they are shown to their bedrooms. These are little wall niches. The boys climb in quickly. But, alas, Babar and Celeste are too big to fit into them. So Blue Mushroom orders the pool emptied and filled with pillows.

"Well, here is a very comfortable place," sighs Celeste, as she settles down. "My, I'm so sleepy!"

Every morning, escorted by the little dog, they all go to the breakfast fountain with Pointed Hat and Blue Mushroom. This is an automatic fountain which serves cakes and soft drinks. All they have to do is push a button to start it. But, if one is not used to such a fountain, it is difficult to aim straight and drink from it properly. Babar is not too good at this....

Babar would very much like to replace his lost shoe. He succeeds in making himself understood, and Pointed Hat takes him to a supermarket with Arthur and Zephir. Babar tries on the biggest pairs in the shop, but he is very disappointed. None of them are large enough for him. He decides to take off his remaining shoe, and walk about in his socks. "It will be more elegant," he says.

Today a splendid festival is being held in the floating city: a tournament of flying eggs. Everyone has gathered in the grandstand to watch the contestants try to unseat each other so they fall down onto the big elastic net.

Arthur is taking part. He pushes his opponent with his pole and succeeds in unseating him! Bravo! He's won! But then Arthur loses his balance and falls into the net, too. He bounces like a ball. "Watch out!" cries Zephir. "Be careful, Arthur!"

Arthur bounces so high that he bumps into his flying egg. The flying egg veers so sharply that the pilot cannot avoid colliding with one of the big red balloons. The balloon rips! The air rushes out! Arthur falls down on the net unharmed, but the terrified spectators get up and rush off screaming.

The punctured balloon gets smaller and smaller. The platform on which Babar and Celeste are sitting tilts dangerously! "Quick, to the emergency ladders!" somebody shouts. Everyone rushes to climb onto another platform.

A siren screeches and Babar sees a strange contraption. A rescue crew
has arrived to replace the collapsed balloon.

"I'd like very much to have a machine like that," Zephir
thinks. "It's like a fire engine." A new balloon is
quickly inflated and hung up to replace the first one.
The platform balances properly again.
The danger is over.

They all meet at the home of Pointed Hat and Blue Mushroom. Arthur has a big lump on his forehead and is still somewhat dazed. The little blue dog tries to comfort him.

But the natives of the soft planet seem annoyed. They frown and complain bitterly. Babar is concerned, and says to himself, "Maybe they think that Arthur burst the balloon on purpose." Pointed Hat also seems worried. "I'll ask him what's the matter," Babar decides. "Maybe I can find out what's going on."

"Are you angry?" Babar asks his friend, for by now they can understand each other better. Pointed Hat hesitates before replying. "I'm not angry. I know perfectly well that what happened to Arthur was an accident. But the others are upset. This might be dangerous for you, my dear Babar. It might be better for you to return to earth. I will be sorry—I, who was the one who made you come all this way because I wanted to get to know you. But I think we had better say farewell . . . until another time."

When night falls, it is parting time, but before leaving the soft planet, Babar receives a gift—an adorable little blue puppy.

The floating city is far away now. Babar and Celeste, Pom, Flora and Alexander, Arthur and Zephir have left as they came—in skimmercraft. Blue Mushroom and Pointed Hat have accompanied them to the rocket. The rocket shoots up into the sky.

Babar looks back pensively at the soft planet, which is getting smaller and smaller.

Back in Celesteville, they are welcomed joyfully by all their friends, who thought that they had perished. The little blue puppy is a great success, but the Old Lady, still very upset, is crying. "Why did they kidnap you so brutally?" she asks.

"They didn't know any other way to invite us to their country," answers Babar.

"But now," adds Arthur, "now that we know them, we can telephone to them and I hope that they will come to see us in Celesteville."

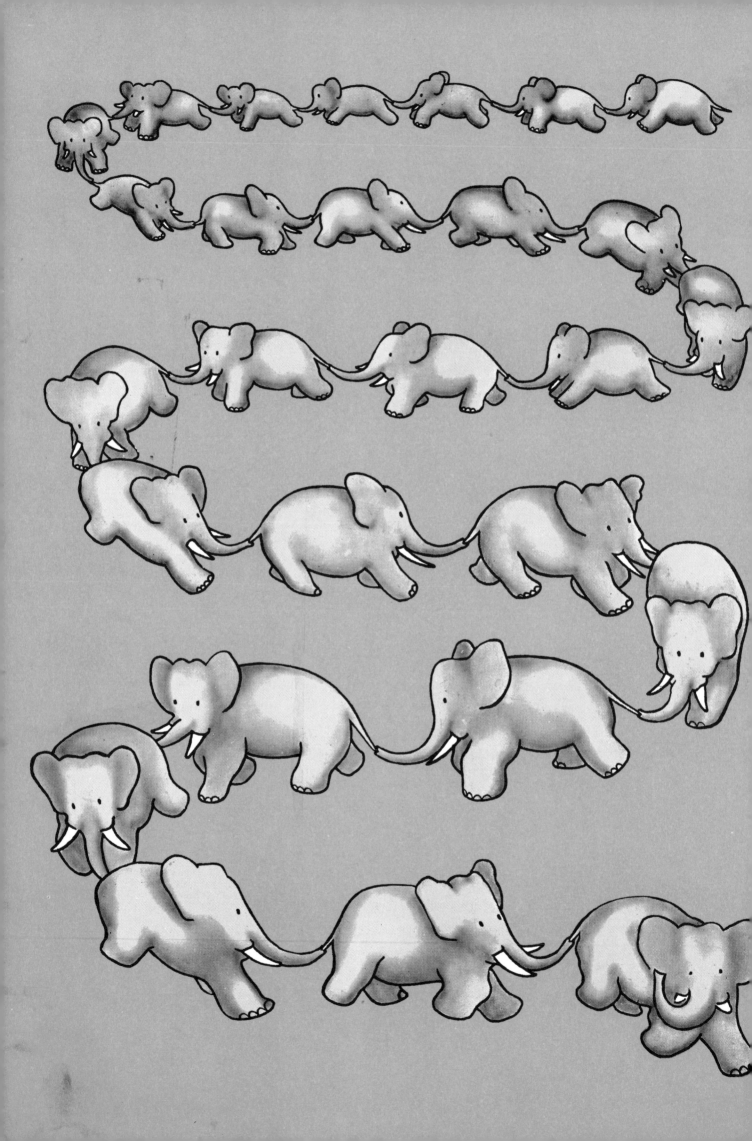